Cyber Age Rhymes

Nursery Rhymes for Smart Kids

Devajit Bhuyan

Ukiyoto Publishing

All global publishing rights are held by

Ukiyoto Publishing

Published in 2024

Content Copyright © Devajit Bhuyan

ISBN 9789367956915

www.ukiyoto.com

This book is dedicated to my wife late Mitali Bhuyan who once worked as a nursery schoolteacher before joining the Guwahati High Court, Assam, India as an Advocate and Notary. She was loved by all kids during her short stint as a nursery teacher. Love you,

Mitali, this is a small gift for your birthday.

Contents

Preface

Technology has given us comfort and luxury. But technology has not been able to give us harmony, peace, and happiness. This is because of the breakdown of our value system. It is high time that we teach our children values along with science & technology from childhood through various means. I think rhymes are a medium which is very suitable for sending a message. We have forgotten most of the poems we read during our school days, but the rhymes we learnt are always fresh.

Most of our schools are still teaching our children rhymes, which have no relevance or very little relevance to our present society, time, and culture. My Cyber Age Rhymes is my second effort in the direction to make rhymes relevant to modern times and our Indian society. Like my previous rhymes book *21ˢᵗ Century Rhymes,* which was accepted well, if readers accept this book, I will think that my effort has not gone in vain.

Place: Guwahati

Date: 02.11.2024
Devajit Bhuyan

Morning

The Sun rises
Good morning comes
Breakfast waits for us
Let me brush first.

Study

Morning shows the day
Cloudy or Sunny
Unless we study hard
Life will be tyranny.

Smartphone

Smartphone phones are very handy
Children love it more than sugar candy
Dog, cat, black sheep everything there
Using smartphone too much not fair
Let's play with pets in the garden
Ignore the smartphone bell as burden.

Website

Websites are clumsy like spiders' net
Good or bad no one can quickly bet
Let us use it only to acquire knowledge
We shall have enough use during college.

Computer

CPU, Keyboard, Mouse and Monitor
All makes a machine
Called the Computer
CPU is the Brain
Key-Board and Mouse hand-feet
Monitor expresses like the mouth
Everything is now on fingertip
Smartphone is a big leap.

Internet

Internet, Internet
Papa, what is it?
A young postman
Without a delivery van
Carries our letter
The weather did not matter!
Travel through fiber line
Gives infotainment very fine
A good teacher
Library in the pocket
The Internet can go anywhere
Without any ticket.

Babbage

Babbage, Babbage
Computer is now big Star
So fast silicon brain
Why travel by train?
When you make the difference engine
Did you ever think?
Computers has changed the World
Different inventions quickly unfold.

Cloud

Cloud can now keep information
Amazon uses cloud computing
Like mouse now has two identities
The pizza box needs real deliveries.

Solar Energy

Fossil fuels destroying environment
Solar energy now so very pertinent
We must work for carbon neutral future
Reduce, recycle should be our culture.

Pollution

Pollution, Pollution
We have a solution!
If we save fuel
The air will not be cruel.

Best Friend

Don't cut a tree
Air it clear
Our best friend
Trees are my dear.

Science

Science and Technology
They are not Mythology
Studying both are must
Respecting the teacher is just.

Space Travel

Now we can easily travel to the moon
Going to the Mars will be reality soon
Space-X is doing good business
To migrate for another planet, I am in readiness.

Kalpana Chawla

Kalpana died at the time of landing
Space shuttle services in the making
She was brave and showed new paths
To be an astronaut important is maths.

Sunita Williams

The brave astronaut still stuck in space
In the space station continuing race
Never become afraid of what happened
Her return was delayed suddenly
Continuing research in space laboratory
She will be known as Sunita legendary.

AI, AI

AI, AI reading and writing goodbye
You have memory infinite and hi fi
Yet to compete with you I will try
Because you have no emotion to cry.

ChatGPT

ChatGPT, Siri all are human tools
You are the master of setting their rules.
Considering them superman are fools
While using them always remain cool.

Online Shoping

Shopping is now so easy
Online stores are too rosy
Shopping from home is cosy
Bad delivery only makes it lousy.

Best Computer

I am the best PC

Brain my Hard Disc

Hand can do all jobs

Mouth for a Kiss

Eyes can see everything

No need of Scanner

Computers can't read even

The biggest banner.

Who Says What

The Clock says tick tick

The phone cring cring

The Cat says mew mew

The grass collects dew

The bell says dingdong

The Dog says vow vow

The teacher says good boy

Standup in the row.

Counting

One, two, three, four, five

Mummy had lost her beautiful knife

Six, seven, eight, nine, ten

Will you give her a new one again?

How much money shall it cost?

My pocket money I have lost

Papa will give it to me again

I will pay you without a bargain.

Time

Time passes every second

The day with the Sun

Seven days a week

Thirty days a month

Twelve months make a year

Ten years a decade

Hundred Years Century take

Few people can make.

Play Time

Afternoon, afternoon
Playtime finishes soon
Homework must be done
I will be second to none.

Twelve Months

January, February, March
Exam approaches very fast
April, May June
Summer vacation finishes soon
July, August, September
Lessons are to be badger
October, November, December
We study hard to remember.

Little Boy

I am a little boy
I love to play with toy
Football and cricket
It also gives joy
He-man, Superman
Barbie and Racing Car
But mummy scolded me
If I play with a water Jar.

Little Girl

I am a little girl
Strong and stout
Flying like butterfly
It is my bout
When the Sun sets
Then I take a rest.

Little Star

Twinkle, Twinkle little star
How many Light Years
Far from us you are
Sun and Moon very near
Hundred times away
You O' dear.
Light is so fast
Yet it takes years
How can I get there
So, you come near.

Birthday

Birthdays come once in a year
That is why it is so dear
Chocolate, Balloon and cake
Memorable days we always make,

Mountain And Sea

Mountain is very tall
So also, the waterfalls,
The sea is very deep
In seas big fishes live
The desert is hot and sandy
Riding a Camel, it is handy,
Rivers are very long
Little Spring sings a song.

River

Amazon, Neil, Mississippi
Brahmaputra, Ganga, Valga
All are nature's lifeline
Let us not pollute them
To make our future fine.

Rainbow

Rainbow, Rainbow
You look like a bow
Seven colors look like a row
VIBGYOR is the name
Violet, Indigo Blue
Green is in the middle
Yellow, Orange, Red then paddle
Together they make a rainbow bundle.

Animal King

Cat and the Rat
Ran around a Hat
Mouse Went to the Ring
Everybody declared him the King
Fox was on the Box
Dog was after the Ox
Lion was drowned
Mouse was so Crowned.

Lovely Deer

O' Deer, O' Deer
Please come near
Never do any evil
Yet people like to kill
So beautiful your charm
We promise you no harm.

Gravity

I was an apple
Hanging from a tree
Something pulled me
To fall free
Newton saw it
Sitting in a garden
Gravity pulled me down
Weight is the burden.

Harmony

Arm in arm
Hand in hand
Let's play
Harmony band
Hindu, Muslim
Christian, Jew, Sikh
Brotherhood our
Foundation Brick.

My Country

Motherland, motherland
I love you
So many languages
Religions, color and creed
Unity is our need
Division gives violence
Lesson of the time
Unity and integrity
Mission our Prime.

Honesty

Money can buy a beautiful toy
But not, Happiness and Joy!
Mother's love not for sale
Honesty and truth never pale.

Good Night

Good night, sleeping time
Sweet dream so fine
No work, no book
Naughty alarms don't look.

Cyber Age Abc

A   FOR   AI (Artificial Intelligence)

B   FOR   BYTE

C   FOR   COMPUTER

D   FOR   DOWNLOAD

E   FOR   E-MAIL

F   FOR   FLOPPY

G   FOR   GOOGLE

H   FOR   HARDWARE

I   FOR   INTERNET

J   FOR   JUNCTION-DIODE

K   FOR   KEYBOARD

L   FOR   LAPTOP

M   FOR   MB (Mega Bytes)

N   FOR   NETWORK

O   FOR   OS (OPERATING SYSTEM)

P   FOR   PENDRIVE

Q   FOR   QUANTUM

R   FOR   RAM

S   FOR   SMARTPHONE

T   FOR   TELEMATICS

U   FOR   UNIX

V   FOR   VIDEO GAME

W   FOR   WEB SITE

X   FOR   XENIX

Y   FOR   YouTube

Z   FOR   ZOOM

About the Author

Devajit Bhuyan

DEVAJIT BHUYAN, an electrical engineer by profession and poet from the heart, is proficient in composing poetry in English and his mother tongue Assamese. His Rhymes book titled "21st Century Rhymes" published during Y2K days is still best-selling Rhymes book in India. His book "Multiple Career Choices" and "A Complete Guide to Career Planning" are still popular among school students. His writings are part of textbook for class-X in Assam under Board of Secondary Education. His books on Kalpana Chawla and on science are popular among young and olds. Till now he has published 209 books in 45 languages. To know more about him please visit www.devajitbhuyan.com.

www.ingramcontent.com/pod-product-compliance
Lightning Source LLC
Chambersburg PA
CBHW021331160726
47994CB00004B/1710